Spooky Classics for Children

AS TOLD BY
JIM WEISS

— A Companion Reader —

With Dramatizations by Chris Bauer

WELL-TRAINED MIND PRESS

Publisher's Cataloging-In-Publication Data
(Prepared by The Donohue Group, Inc.)
Names: Weiss, Jim. | Wilde, Oscar, 1854–1900. Canterville ghost. | Hawthorne, Nathaniel, 1804–1864. Dr. Heidegger's experiment. | Kipling, Rudyard, 1865–1936. Sending of Dana Da. | Bauer, Chris, 1991–screenwriter.
Title: Spooky classics for children : a companion reader / as told by Jim Weiss ; with dramatizations by Chris Bauer.
Description: [Charles City, Virginia] : Well-Trained Mind Press, [2016] | Interest age level: 7 and up. | A word-for-word transcript of the original audiobook produced: Benicia, CA : Greathall Productions, 1997. | Summary: Contains adaptations of three spooky tales from Wilde, Hawthorne and Kipling. The stories are followed by three dramatizations that children can perform on their own or together.
Identifiers: LCCN 2016947142 | ISBN 978-1-933339-96-2
Subjects: LCSH: Ghost stories. | Elixirs-- Juvenile fiction. | CYAC: Ghosts-- Fiction. | Elixirs-- Fiction. | LCGFT: Paranormal fiction. | Children's plays.
Classification: LCC PN6071.G45 W45 2016 | DDC 808.83/8733-- dc23

For a complete list of history and language arts materials published by Well-Trained Mind Press, along with many more Jim Weiss titles, visit welltrainedmind.com.

Contents

Preface

This illustrated Companion Reader is an exact transcript of Jim Weiss's award-winning storytelling performance, *Spooky Classics for Children*.

For decades, Jim Weiss has entertained his many listeners with gripping plots, vivid characters, and beautiful words. But his performances are much more than mere entertainment. Jim's stories build language skills by filling young minds with wonderful vocabulary, complex sentence structures, and rich images.

Now, our Companion Readers bring these language-learning benefits to a new level. Language, both written and oral, is most easily and thoroughly learned when *heard, read,* and *spoken*.

Listen to the Jim Weiss performance on CD or MP3. (See well-trainedmind.com for a full listing and instantly downloadable digital versions!)

Read along with the performance. The first half of this book is a word-for-word transcript of Jim Weiss's performance. Students can improve their reading fluency, vocabulary, and their understanding of punctuation, sentence structure, and grammar by following along as Jim performs these words. Even students who are not reading at the level represented in this book can be moved forward in reading competency by reading along as Jim speaks the words.

Note: To help you follow along with the audio performance, we've placed Track Numbers into the text wherever a new track begins on the CD or MP3 recording. They look like this:

TRACK 1

Say the words. The final element in language learning is to speak great words and sentences out loud. Each one of these performances has been turned into a short, accessible dramatic version that can be performed by two or more actors. The plays can be memorized or read from the scripts; either way, students will begin to gain confidence in their own language use and in their ability to speak in front of others.

Each play has a slightly different emphasis. The first, *The Canterville Ghost*, gives students an opportunity to practice different kinds of simple special effects. The second, *Dr. Heidegger's Experiment*, focuses on physical acting: walking and moving as characters of different ages, as well as "pretend" stage fighting. The third, *The Sending of Dana Da*, guides young actors in interacting with a live audience.

PART I:
THREE SPOOKY STORIES

Oscar Wilde's
The Canterville Ghost
As Told by Jim Weiss

There's something about a spooky story that draws us in, and holds us for the most startling developments. Here, from three masters of literature, are three spooky classics.

The author of *The Canterville Ghost,* Oscar Wilde, grew up in Ireland and then later made his name as a writer in London, England. There, Wilde created plays, essays, poems, short stories, and a famous novel, all filled with sparkling wit. Beneath the entertainment, however, lay a first-rate mind seeking real meaning in existence and human relationships.

The Canterville Ghost is one of a collection of stories in which Oscar Wilde blended fantasy and the supernatural with his brilliant comments on human nature.

The Canterville Ghost
by Oscar Wilde

Everyone told Hiram B. Otis that he was making the mistake of his life, and they meant what they said. Mr. Otis, the self-made millionaire businessman, had been appointed the new American ambassador to Great Britain, and although he had no use for what he considered the fancy airs of British aristocrats, he told his wife, "We shall have to live in such a manner that they will respect my position. And so, my dear, we need a house."

And that's how Mr. and Mrs. Otis came to buy that famous old ancestral castle, Canterville Chase.

There was just one problem: Canterville Chase was haunted.

Everyone warned them. Mrs. Otis, a celebrated beauty with a marvelously dry sense of humor, found the warnings amusing. "You found us a place that's haunted?" she asked her husband with a dazzling smile. "Hiram, how charming!"

Even Lord Canterville tried to tell them about it: "You see, it's been some years since we Cantervilles have lived at the old place ourselves. We stuck it out for generations—centuries, in fact—ever since the ghost of my ancestor, Sir Simon de Canterville, first appeared. He has been seen frequently through the years, and to quite terrifying effect. What finally cut it for us was the evening my grand-aunt, the Dowager Duchess of Bolton, felt two skeletal hands on her shoulders as she was dressing for dinner. And I assure you, she was the last person on earth who would imagine such things."

And that seemed to Lord Canterville to be the last word on the subject.

Mr. Otis thanked him for his good intentions, but said, "We'll take the place and everything in it, including the furniture and the servants. I don't wish to sound rude, my lord, but I represent a modern nation. We don't believe in any superstitious mumbo-jumbo we can't understand. (Except maybe for Congress.) We'll take our chances with this ghost business."

And so the Otis family, believers in democracy, progress, and the American Way, came to Canterville Chase.

There were four children in the family, three of them boys. The oldest had been named Washington by his civic-minded parents. The youngest were the energetic twins, who were as patriotic as their father and so were usually referred to as Stars and Stripes. "A castle?" the boys shouted when they heard about their new home. "We're going to live in a castle?" And they whooped and hollered.

Their sister, Miss Virginia E. Otis, was a bit more reserved in her remarks. Virginia was a quiet, self-assured young lady, although she could be as high-spirited as her brothers when provoked. Why, once in London when old Lord Bilton made some disparaging remarks about American horses, she firmly replied, "I beg your pardon, my pony can outrace your horse any day." And she raced him twice around Kensington Palace, winning by a length and a half. The young Duke of Cheshire (who watched the whole thing) thought her completely marvelous, and he wondered whether he

should become the first in his family to marry someone from outside his native shores.

When the Otis family arrived at Canterville Chase they found the housekeeper, Mrs. Umney, waiting on the wide front steps. "I bid you welcome to your new home at Canterville Chase," she said, ushering them in.

The Otises were soon seated in the wood-paneled library, sipping tea before a low fire. Mrs. Otis noticed a dull red stain on the floor by the fireplace, and she said to the housekeeper, "Mrs. Umney, it seems something has been spilled there. Would you be kind enough to see to it?"

"Oh, madam," replied the housekeeper, "I'm afraid that what's been spilt there cannot be removed so easily as all that. It's blood. It was on that very spot that Sir Simon de Canterville murdered his wife, the Lady Eleanore, many centuries ago. He himself disappeared a few years later, and was never seen again. Or at least . . . he was never seen alive. His guilty spirit still haunts this estate. And as for the bloodstain, well, it's been removed before, but it always returns. I tell you, 'tis no easy thing to live at Canterville Chase. There are those it has driven to madness!"

"Nonsense!" exclaimed Washington, the oldest Otis boy. "Whoever dealt with this stain before didn't have all the modern conveniences! We'll just take it out with a little bit of Pinkerton's Champion Stain Remover!"

And to Mrs. Umney's surprise, Washington produced a dark-colored stick from his coat pocket which he proceeded to rub on the bloodstain. "There! All gone! Pinkerton's always does the trick, no matter how old the stain may be!"

The next morning, however, they found the bloodstain back on the library floor.

"That's funny," said Washington. "Pinkerton's has always worked perfectly." He rubbed out the stain again, but it was back the next day, and no matter how often he removed it, it was back the next day and the next—even when Mr. Otis took to locking the library door at night.

And then, late one night, hours after the family had fallen asleep in their large four-poster beds, Mr. Otis awoke, quite suddenly, to a loud metallic clanking in the corridor. He sat up, quietly donned his slippers and robe so as not to awaken his wife, drew a small bottle from his dresser drawer, and opened the bedroom door.

Then he stopped in his tracks, for not five feet away from him, lit eerily by moonlight through the hall window, was a horrible vision! It was an old man dressed in ancient-looking ragged clothes, and with matted grey hair fallen to his shoulders. His eyes blazed as red as two lumps of coal in the midst of a face pale as the moonlight. Hanging from his wrists and dragging from his ankles were heavy-looking locks and chains made of rusted metal. The spectral visitor turned and stared straight at Mr. Otis, and a strange bubbling sound issued from its throat. Its movement shifted the locks and chains, producing the noise Mr. Otis had heard in his room.

Mr. Otis drew a deep breath and said, "My dear sir, if you are going to move through our home wearing those chains I must insist that you oil them. We need our sleep, especially the children. Therefore, I have taken the liberty of bringing you this little bottle of Tammany Rising Sun Metal Lubricator, made in the U.S. of A. Just a small amount properly applied should do the trick. Thank you and good evening."

And setting the bottle down on a marble table, the ambassador returned to his room, closing the door.

The Canterville Ghost stood a moment, unmoving, glaring at the closed door. Then he dashed the bottle to the floor (where it shattered against the table leg), turned, and flew down the hallway. But just as he reached the top of the huge main staircase, the Otis twins, clad in nightshirts, appeared in their doorway and let loose with their pillows, which whizzed past the ghost's head.

With a startled exclamation he stopped. Then he turned, took a deep breath, and let loose with a peel of maniacal laughter: "HAHAHAHAHAHAHAHA-HAAAAA!" The horrid sound echoed off the high ceiling and walls.

As it died away, Mrs. Otis, awake at last, appeared in her doorway. She looked at the ghost with concern on her face and said, "My goodness, you don't sound at all well. If you'll just give me a moment I can offer you some of Doctor Dobell's Miracle Cure, which is absolutely the thing for stomach ailments or influenza."

The ghost's red eyes lit even more brightly, and he was just drawing a breath to turn himself into a huge vicious-looking black hound, when he heard a noise behind him, turned, and noticed the twins sneaking towards him, carrying pea shooters. So instead he began to glow a sickly green, and then faded away. The last they saw of him was the two red eyes, glowing in the air for several seconds before they too disappeared.

The Canterville Ghost thrust himself hurriedly through the walls of the old house and reappeared at last in a concealed chamber far from the Otises' bedrooms. Throwing himself into a chair, which could be seen right through him, he sat catching his breath. Then anger began to boil up in him.

"What is this world coming to?" he asked himself. "Why, in over three centuries of haunting I have never been so insulted, so ill used, so ignored!" To reassure himself of his longstanding skills, he went to his desk and lifted up his diary, a large volume with a dark leather cover. He opened to one of his favorite entries.

"This evening I had a most gratifying encounter with Reverend Dampier, the local clergyman, who had had the temerity to doubt my existence. Well—after tonight he will doubt no more! As he left the castle library, I followed him into the hallway and blew out his candle, and then each time he lit it again I extinguished it again, until he ran through the darkened halls, screaming and bumping into the furniture in such fear that I had to stop pursuing him because I was laughing too hard."

He went on to review others of his most celebrated performances, including his famous turn as Red Reuben, the Fiend From Beyond the Grave, and that marvelous time he had panicked an entire party of picnickers while done up as Gaunt Gideon, The Bloodsucker of Bexley Moor.

"Why," he concluded, "I am absolutely at the top of my profession. In all this part of England there is no ghostly spirit half so versatile or with half my reputation." And he began to perk up again.

There was no further sign of the Canterville Ghost for a time, except for the reappearance every day of the bloodstain on the library carpet. Oddly, the stain was a different color every other day or so, ranging from a true deep red through a sort of purplish red to a deep purple, and reaching a sort of culmination when one morning they found it a bright emerald green. "As if," Mrs. Otis said to her husband, "the blood came from someone Irish." He smiled, but Mrs. Otis noticed their daughter Virginia was growing increasingly upset with each change of color.

The next few days passed quietly enough, but this was merely the lull before the storm. In the past, the mere appearance of the Canterville Ghost had been enough to frighten anyone. These newcomers were a different sort altogether, and the ghost had determined to meet the challenge. He was only taking his time, carefully planning a grand and truly terrifying appearance. He told himself, "This will send them hurrying back to the colonies on the next ship!"

Poetically, he chose Friday the 13th for this offensive. He spent all day preparing his wardrobe and makeup. He recorded his plan in his diary: "I have settled upon the combination of Bloody Hans, the Butcher of Hamburg, with the always effective Desolate Prince." This meant he would appear as a green, icy cold corpse dressed in old bloody clothing and wrapped half around with grave cloths. These he would slowly unwind with one hand while flourishing a rusty dagger with the other. "And then my supreme moment; having removed the bloody grave cloths I stand revealed in the form of . . . a skeleton! With bleached white bones . . . and, I think . . . yes, just one rolling eyeball." (This was one of those effects he saved for really special occasions).

He would start with Washington Otis, against whom he held a special grudge for cleaning up the blood-stain each day. ("Pinkerton's Champion Stain Remover indeed! I'll give him something he can't remove so easily!") And then, when Washington was in the very throes of fear, the ghost would melt away through the wall into the parents' room.

Finally, the ghost would reach the pinnacle of his efforts with a direct attack on the twins, the worst offenders of all. "How satisfying!" he thought. He hadn't quite settled on anything for the young lady Virginia, who had never insulted him or treated him shabbily, and who besides somehow reminded him of his own mother. He thought he might just appear in her mirror and moan a few times, which he practiced after warming up his throat a bit: "Ahem. Oooooh! Ooooooooooh! Hmm, perhaps in a higher key . . . oooooooooh!"

And so, having laid his plans, he waited until the great old clock in the upstairs hall struck midnight. Then the Canterville Ghost left his place in the shadows to strike terror into the hearts of the unsuspecting Otis family.

Silently he stole through the hallway towards Washington's room. He turned the corner . . . and let out a

terrible wail of terror, leaping backwards, for there in front of him was a dreadful sight! It was a thing with a bald head and pale white face, eyes and mouth that seemed to be on fire, and clothing as torn and hideous as his own. Around its neck was a hangman's noose, from which there dangled a piece of cardboard covered with twisted letters!

The whole thing was so frightening that he turned to escape, but just then two small figures leaped in his way and shouted "Boo! Boo!"

Seized with panic, and blocked in both directions, he rushed through a partially open doorway, but as he flung it open a heavy jug of water crashed down on him, drenching him completely. Springing forward into the fireplace, in which fortunately no fire was burning, he flung himself up the chimney and back to his secret room.

Once there he threw himself down, gasping for breath. At last after a few moments the old Canterville courage arose and he determined to go back. "This is my haunting place," he told himself. "I am not about to surrender it to some Johnny-come-lately spirit. Besides, if I can convince the other ghost to join forces with me, together we might frighten away these Otises at last."

So you can imagine his reaction when he returned to the scene only to find that the horrible vision had been constructed from a white sheet, a long-handled broom, a hollow white turnip, and a now-melted candle. Worst of all, the sign that had hung from the so-called ghost's neck carried these words: "Ye Otis Ghost, Ye Only True and Original Spooke. Beware of Ye Imitations."

As the Canterville Ghost read these words, something went out of him. Slowly he dragged his way back to his room, slumped in his chair, and sat unmoving.

The next day he decided that he would no longer replenish the bloodstain on the library floor. He told himself, "If these barbarians don't appreciate it, they don't deserve it."

He did determine to resume his activities several weeks later when Virginia Otis's young suitor, the Duke of Cheshire, came to visit from his own nearby estate. Through the years the ghost had terrified three previous Dukes of Cheshire, and he felt a sort of pride of ownership toward that family. In the end, however, picturing the Otis twins lying in wait, the ghost couldn't quite summon up the necessary resolve. And so the adoring young Duke was able to spend time with Virginia undisturbed.

On their horseback ride over the estate, Virginia tore her riding jacket on a branch and they rode back to the house. "Edward," she told the Duke, leaving him in the drawing room, "I'll just run up and change my outfit." But upstairs, as she hurried by the tapestry room, she saw her father sitting, staring out the window. Then she took a second look and saw that it was not her father at all but the ghost of Sir Simon de Canterville. She noticed that he had the saddest expression on his face.

Kind-hearted soul that she was, Virginia felt sorry for him. She had removed her muddy riding boots and was in her stocking feet, so the ghost did not hear her approaching.

"I'm very sorry for all the trouble," she began, "but if you'll just be patient a few more days, my brothers and I will be going off to school. Then, if you'll behave yourself, no one will bother you."

The ghost looked with astonishment at this young girl who addressed him so calmly. And he said, "Well, really, it's no good asking me to 'behave myself.' It is my job to moan and rattle chains and all the rest that goes with it. If I cannot do these things I've simply no reason to exist. But thank you for your concern."

"It's just common decency," replied Virginia. "Really, I'm quite annoyed with you. You had no right to steal my paints from my paint box to refurbish your dreadful bloodstain. First you took all my reds, then you took my purples so I couldn't even paint any more sunsets, which are my favorites. And then you took my greens, and I'd never done anything to you! Besides, Mrs. Umney told us the day we arrived that you had killed your wife."

"Perfectly true," he admitted. "Oh, but it was a different world then. We medieval lords were the masters— not only of our own lives, we ruled also the lives of all those around us. I'm afraid I grew so caught up in my role as lord of this place that I would not tolerate the least provocation from anyone else. One day my wife and I had a difference of opinion and I struck her."

"You didn't!" exclaimed Virginia.

"Yes, I did. And she lost her balance and fell, and struck her head on the stones at the foot of the fireplace there in the library. She was dead on the instant. I felt dreadful but of course there was nothing to be done. I had loved her, you know. I took to wandering the estate at all hours of the day and night, and when, a few years later, I too crossed over—"

"When you died, you mean?"

"Well . . . there's the problem you see. I never died, quite. I had experienced such guilt that instead of finding eternal peace I was condemned to walk these halls forever." He sighed and looked up at her, smiling sadly. "Do you know I haven't slept in over three hundred years?"

"No! Not really?"

"Indeed. If only I could sleep . . . if I could forget the pain I caused others and myself with the sins of my life . . . do you know, child, I sometimes think I might once again find her and beg her forgiveness, and then I would truly rest in peace."

Virginia asked, "Is there no hope for you?" And then, before he could reply, she answered herself: "Yes, there must always be hope."

This caused the ghost to look at her intently, and he said, "Perhaps you could open the doorway for me. I have seen you during these weeks. Love is always with you, and love is stronger than death itself. You, child, who are so filled with compassion for others, you who have boundless faith, faith enough even to believe that an old accursed spirit such as I might yet be saved . . . you might hold a vision of hope for me still. And if you weep, and if you pray, perhaps I too will remember how, and the angel of death might have mercy on me. Oh, but you will see fearful shapes and visions in the darkness, and hear terrifying voices warning you to abandon your hope. There are always such voices in the world, Virginia. But if you are brave and persist, they cannot harm you, for they've no real power over the faith of a loving heart."

He looked intently at her, and she did not move for a long moment. At last she said quietly, "Let us try."

He cried out, and rising from his chair he bent his head low to kiss her hand. Then he led her across the room toward the largest woven tapestry, which covered an entire wall. He raised his hand, and the tapestry rose up, and the wall behind slid to the side. She saw a great darkness behind it, and a cold wind blew harshly at her from inside, a wind filled with swirling voices, yet still she moved forward.

And with the ghost of Sir Simon de Canterville at her side, Virginia stepped through.

A moment later, the wall slid back into place, the tapestry fell as it had been, and all was silent in the room.

About ten minutes later, the silence was broken by a bell ringing through the house, summoning the Otis family to afternoon tea. Their guest, the Duke of

Cheshire, was disturbed when Virginia did not appear with the others, but not until dinnertime did they feel real alarm. For hours they searched the house and the grounds, and Mr. Otis had just declared he would call in the police when the old upstairs clock began to chime midnight. As its last stroke ended, they heard a dreadful cry, and then beautiful, unearthly music began to fill the old house. A panel at the top of the staircase slid back, and there stood Virginia. She stepped through the opening, and they all ran up and began to speak at once.

Virginia turned her gaze upon each of them in turn and then announced, "I'm so sorry to have worried you. I was with Sir Simon."

"What!" they exclaimed.

"Yes. I had a long talk with him. He lived quite a wicked life, I'm afraid, and he felt so badly about it afterward that he couldn't sleep for the longest time. He asked me if I could help him, and I did. And now at last he can rest. She has forgiven him. And look, before he died he gave me this box of beautiful jewels to keep!" And she looked straight at the young Duke of Cheshire and smiled.

Well, there's little more to tell, but what there is is worth telling. Mr. Otis insisted that Lord Canterville

receive back the magnificent jewels the ghost had given to Virginia, saying "These are Canterville jewels, after all."

But his lordship held up a hand and replied, "My dear sir, if you'll recall, when you acquired Canterville Chase you acquired everything in it. These are quite properly yours, and from what you tell me the young lady certainly earned them. Besides, the old fellow . . . you know whom I mean . . . gave them to her himself. I suspect that if I was so rash as to receive them from you he'd be out of his grave and paying me rather a nasty visit before the week was out. No, I insist they stay with your daughter."

And so they did, although it was some years before she had the opportunity to wear them. On that memorable occasion, both she and her jewels were the subject of profound admiration as the young lady was presented at court to good Queen Victoria herself.

"Your majesty!" said the Duke of Cheshire, "May I have the pleasure of presenting to you Virginia—my wife."

Nathaniel Hawthorne's
Dr. Heidegger's Experiment
As Told by Jim Weiss

Nathaniel Hawthorne lived in Concord, Massachusetts, in the early 1800s. His neighbors there included Louisa May Alcott, Henry David Thoreau, and Ralph Waldo Emerson, all famous authors, and all friends who encouraged each other's writing. Hawthorne's keen observations of human strengths and weaknesses made him an honored member of this group. Here, then, is one example of his genius.

Dr. Heidegger's Experiment,
by Nathaniel Hawthorne

The four guests, seated around the table in the curious old-fashioned chamber, waited for their host to explain what he was up to *this* time.

There were three white-haired gentlemen—Mr. Medbourne, Colonel Killigrew, and Mr. Gascoigne—and an elderly widow, Widow Wycherly. They had known each other forever, and each knew the misfortunes that had happened to the others on the way to old age.

Mr. Medbourne had been a prosperous merchant, but he had gambled it all on some wild business dealings and lost everything.

Mr. Gascoigne was a ruined politician with a reputation for dishonesty—or at least that had been his reputation until so many years passed that the new generation had forgotten completely about him.

Colonel Killigrew? Well, perhaps the less said about him, the better. Let's just say that in his younger days, if there was some sin to be found, he'd be the one to find it. Now he was paying for all that with discomforts in his body and his soul.

As for the Widow Wycherly, she had been one of the great beauties of her time, but that time was long past. She kept to herself mostly, and the leading citizens in town steered clear of her because of the scandalous stories that still followed her from her youth. It's worth mentioning that all three of the old gentlemen (Medbourne, Gascoigne, and Killigrew) had been in love with her as young men, and only age had softened their violent rivalry for her.

So these were the four guests seated around the table in the curious old-fashioned study of that curious old-fashioned gentleman, Dr. Heidegger. He was their host.

And now that they were seated he said to them, "My dear old friends, I've asked you here today in hope that you will assist me in one of those little experiments with which I amuse myself here in my study." On the circular table around which they now sat, the doctor had placed a clear vase of elegantly cut glass. By chance, the sunshine through it cast a deep color across their faces, as he set before them four champagne glasses and said: "I have something to show you."

And then, from between two pages in an old leather book, he drew out what had once been a rose. Its green

leaves and crimson petals were all one shade of brown now, and it looked as if it might crumble into dust in his hands. "This rose," he sighed, "blossomed 55 years ago. It was given to me by Sylvia, whose portrait hangs there." And he nodded with his head to the painting of his true love. "For 55 years it has rested between the pages of this book. Now looking at it, would you think it possible that this rose should ever bloom again?"

"Nonsense," said the Widow Wycherly, tossing back her head. "You might as well ask if an old woman's wrinkled face could bloom again."

But the Doctor replied, "Look!" And, uncovering the glass vase, he dropped the rose into it. It floated upon the surface of the liquid for a few moments, and then something began to change! The dry petals suddenly took on a moist look, and then the crimson color began to deepen while the stalk and the leaves grew green.

"Marvelous!" applauded the Doctor's friends, who assumed it was some sort of illusion or magic trick. "How did you do it?"

He solemnly replied, "Have you ever heard of the Fountain of Youth, which Ponce de Leon, the Spanish explorer, searched for two or three centuries ago?"

"But did Ponce de Leon ever find it?" asked Mr. Medbourne.

"No, for he looked in the wrong place. I'm told it lies in Southern Florida, not far from Lake Macaco. By its springs are century-old trees which, drinking its waters, never grow old. Through a roundabout set of events, this vase has come to me, full of the waters of the Fountain of Youth."

Colonel Killigrew (who didn't believe a word of all this) cleared his throat and asked, "Very useful for a flower, Doctor, but tell me, how would this liquid affect a human being?"

"You shall judge for yourself, Colonel. All of you shall judge for yourselves. You are welcome to as much of this wondrous water as you need in order to restore to you the bloom of youth. As for me, having encountered so much trouble growing old I'm in no hurry to grow young again. With your permission, I'll simply observe the progress of the experiment."

And as they sat in astonishment, he filled the four champagne glasses with the water from the Fountain of Youth. Little bubbles began to rise to the surface, and continued to do so without stopping. A pleasant aroma spread through the room, and almost at the same moment each of them reached out to lift a glass.

"Wait," said Dr. Heidegger. "Before you drink, my respectable old friends, consider for a moment the lives you have lived. With all this experience, wouldn't it be fitting to write up some general rules for your guidance in navigating, for a second time, through the perils of youth? Why waste the wisdom of a lifetime? You could live a wise and virtuous life, and set a fine example for other young people."

But his four elderly friends only laughed feebly, and Mr. Medbourne spoke for them all when he replied, "Why, we should hardly need a list of reminders, Doctor. Surely we would know better this time!" And he reached again for his glass.

"Very well, then," said the Doctor, casting an odd look from one of them to the next. "Drink."

With shaking hands, they lifted their glasses to their lips and drank. Almost at once there was some sort of change, as if the sunshine in the room had suddenly grown brighter on their faces. They looked at one another in astonishment, feeling something moving through their veins, something they began to recall like the melody of an old song long forgotten. The Widow adjusted her cap. She felt almost healthy again for the first time in years.

"Give us more!" she said, and the others all agreed: "Yes, we are younger, but we are still too old! Give us more! Hurry!"

"Patience," counseled the Doctor. "It has taken you a long time to grow old. Surely you can wait half an hour to grow young." But then, seeing their faces, he said, "Very well, then. The water is at your service." And he refilled their glasses.

They drank the liquid at once, and they seemed to feel its effects even as it was running down their throats. They looked at each other. The silvery white was disappearing from their hair, to be replaced by the colors of their youth. Their eyes grew clear and bright. They sat around the table now, three middle-aged gentlemen and a woman hardly beyond her prime.

"My dear Widow!" exclaimed Colonel Killigrew, who had been watching as the years dropped away from her. "You are absolutely charming!"

Now, even though it had been a long time, Widow Wycherly remembered that not all of Colonel Killigrew's compliments could be believed. So she stood up and raced to the mirror, afraid that she she would still see the face that had stared back at her that morning from her own looking-glass at home. She stood before the mirror now and gazed at herself with a devotion she had never wasted on a man. She curtsied and turned this way and that, greeting her image as the friend in all the world of whom she was most fond.

Meanwhile, the three men were proving the effects of the wonderful elixir they had drunk.

Mr. Gascoigne was carrying on, full bore, on all sorts of political subjects. "And I tell you Medbourne, it's not too late as long as there are true patriots about, men and women who are unashamed of their devotion to the flag! Now what this country needs—"

But Mr. Medbourne was hardly listening. He had drawn a pen and paper from Dr. Heidegger's desk and was busily calculating in dollars and cents the cost and the profits involved in a complicated scheme to supply ice to India by harnessing a team of whales to draw down polar icebergs.

As for Colonel Killigrew, he was waltzing around the room and singing a jolly song: "He floats through the air with the greatest of ease, the daring young man on the flying trapeze!" But although he tried to draw the others into a song, they were not interested.

Meanwhile, the Widow Wycherly was still pirou-
etting before the mirror. At last she turned away, and
avoiding for the moment being caught up in a waltz
with the Colonel, she cried, "My dear old Doctor, let's
have another glass!"

"Certainly, my dear madam," he replied. "You see, I
have already filled the glasses."

He watched as they drank for the third time. In a
moment the exhilarating feeling of youth was upon
them. "We are young!" they cried, "We are young!"

The Widow Wycherly sashayed up to the Doctor's
chair with mischief in her eye and cried, "Doctor, you
dear old soul! Get up and dance with me!" Then all four
laughed at the idea.

"Pray excuse me," said Dr. Heidegger. "I am old,
and my dancing days are long gone. But I am sure any
of these young gentlemen," and he waved his hand,
"would be delighted to dance with so lovely a partner."

"Yes, dance with me, Clara!" cried Colonel Killigrew.

"No, no, she shall dance with me!" cried Mr. Gascoigne.

"She promised me her hand fifty years ago!"
exclaimed Mr. Medbourne.

They rushed up to her. While one caught hold of her
hands, another threw an arm about her waist, while the

third buried his hands in her glossy hair. Laughing, panting, they struggled and argued with each other, while the lady laughed in turn with each, pretending to want to free herself and yet not really trying.

Then the laughter turned to argument, and the three men began to fight in earnest. All three lost their balance and struck against the table, which overturned. The vase flew off and shattered into a thousand pieces. The precious water of youth spilled out onto the floor, flowing before the chair in which the Doctor sat, unmoving.

"Come, come, gentlemen. And you too, lady," he scolded. "Look what you have done!"

They stopped. They stared. And then each of them shivered, for an odd feeling was overtaking them. They looked at one another, and then at the old Doctor, who still held in his hand the half-century old rose. He was looking at it closely. "My dear Sylvia's rose . . . it appears to be fading again."

Sure enough, the rose began to shrivel up until at last it was once again as dry and fragile as when he had first taken it from its place among the pages of memory. "I love it just as well this way," said the Doctor softly.

His guests shivered again. Suddenly they felt not only a sort of chill, but a great weariness. As they looked at each other, with each moment there was a change. A wrinkle appeared, a golden hair disappeared to be replaced by white—and in a matter of moments, there in the study before the Doctor's chair stood four old people.

"No! No!" cried Mr. Medbourne.

"Not so soon!" pleaded Mr. Gascoigne to the Doctor who sat, still unmoving.

The Colonel said nothing, but the Widow Wycherly saw him glance at her and turn sharply away, and that moment pierced her heart.

She turned to Dr. Heidegger. "Am I . . . are we old again?" she asked.

"Yes. Yes, you are old again. And the water of youth is gone. And as for me, I am not sorry. If the Fountain itself gushed by my doorstep I would not bathe in it. Such is the lesson you have taught me."

But perhaps the Doctor's four friends were not so wise, for they learned no such lesson. They agreed to set off the next day for Florida in search of the elusive Fountain of Youth, and to find it and to drink from it morning, noon, and night. Full of their plans, they hobbled out into the evening, leaning on each other for support.

The Doctor watched them go. Then he turned back, and gently replaced the rose between the pages of a book.

Rudyard Kipling's
The Sending of Dana Da
As Told by Jim Weiss

The British author Rudyard Kipling lived and wrote in the late 1800s and early 1900s. From his many world travels came exciting novels, short stories, and poems that earned him the Nobel Prize for Literature—and lasting fame. Kipling's lifelong fascination with India became the basis for many of his best-known stories and poems; *The Sending of Dana Da* tells how an Indian and an Englishman share a strange adventure.

The Sending of Dana Da
by Rudyard Kipling

He claimed he was a prophet . . . sometimes. He claimed he was a wizard . . . frequently. He claimed he could tell fortunes . . . always.

His name was Dana Da, which (like everything else about him) was a bit of a mystery. "I am Dana Da," was all he would say, although neither the first nor the last name fit a native of India, which he certainly seemed to be. But he refused to give any more information on the subject.

When the Englishman Richard Evans saw him again—after some years—Dana Da was indeed telling fortunes. This was in the marketplace of a city in Northern India, and Da was plying this questionable trade with the help of a dirty little cloth, some loaded dice whose numbers he could control, and other equally unholy items. He shrugged and explained the necessity of this to Richard Evans by saying simply, "One must live, and I am in reduced circumstances." Although as far as Evans knew, he had never lived any differently.

They had met years ago, and at the time Evans had liked him. Out of kindness he allowed Dana Da to tell

his fortune, providing an excuse to give the fellow some money and a good dinner. Afterwards Dana Da thanked Evans and asked, "Now that you have helped me, how may I help you? Is there anyone you love, for instance, whose love I may help you to obtain?"

Richard Evans couldn't think of a thing. He enjoyed his work, he was in excellent health, and he and his wife already loved each other dearly, so he preferred not to drag her into this.

"Well, then," asked Dana Da, "is there anyone you hate?"

Hesitatingly, Richard Evans replied, "I have to admit there is someone . . . "

He had in mind another Englishman who had so mistreated him as to become his enemy, and who had never given him reason to change his mind.

"Excellent!" said Dana Da. "I will dispatch a sending to him. It will absolutely kill him."

Now, a sending is a horrible arrangement. It's a sort of magical cloud of power that a wizard creates and shapes into, say, a horse or a man (or whatever the wizard decides), and it has such terribly bad energy that it can kill—or at least all this is what superstitious folks think. (It's one reason they rarely tangle with their local wizards.)

"Let me dispatch a sending," said Dana Da. "My own health is sinking fast, but I should like to do this before I go. Because you are my friend, it will cost you only five rupees. What is the name of your enemy?"

Richard Evans mumbled the fellow's name: "Everett Lone."

"Ahh," smiled Dana Da. "I know this man. Once, long ago, he insulted my powers. I should like it to be he."

Now, Richard Evans was not a superstitious man, but he was just unsure enough to say, "Look here, Da, I don't want the fellow dead. Couldn't you just . . . well, I don't know, make his life miserable without doing him any real damage?"

Dana Da replied, "Ah yes, but that is more expensive than killing him. It takes greater control, you see. That will cost you ten rupees. I am not what I once was, and sadly I must take the money."

Richard Evans handed over the ten rupees to him. With great ceremony, Dana Da spread out his rug and lay down on it. Then he closed his eyes, moaned a few times, and went stiff as a board. After about thirty seconds, suddenly he sneezed, then snorted, then sighed. Opening his eyes, he sat up and declared, "The sending has begun. Everett Lone hates cats. Therefore, the sending will take the form of cats. We must send him a letter saying that because he has insulted you and doubted me, a power is directed against him. And soon after he will learn that we speak the truth."

Richard Evans promised more money if the sending came to anything. Then he sent a letter to Everett Lone, dictated by Dana Da, warning in most mysterious terms that something was about to happen. In fact, the letter was so vague and so mysterious that it didn't make much sense, which made it seem even more important.

After he got it, Everett Lone read it over several times and was still in the process of trying to figure out what the dickens it meant when his servant rushed in and told him, "Sir, there is a cat on your bed!"

Now, Everett Lone did hate cats. They were never allowed in, or even around, his home. Furthermore, he knew for a fact that the door of his bedroom had been shut all morning, so no cat could've gotten in.

Still, looking down at the letter he held in his hand, he went to look for himself. With his servant behind him he opened his door. Sure enough, on his bed there lay a white kitten so tiny that it was barely able to lift its head. It took one look at him and said,

"Meow."

Lone told his servant, "Take it away, then change my bed linens. And see to it that this doesn't happen again."

"Yes sir," replied the servant.

But that night as he was reading in his favorite chair, Everett Lone saw a movement out of the corner of his eye just outside the circle of lamplight. Then, again, he heard . . .

"Meow."

He angrily called for his servant, who soon lifted from the shadows a small grey kitten.

"How did this thing get in here?" demanded Lone.

The servant replied, "I promise, sir, it was not here when I came to turn on your lamp. Besides, real kittens don't stray far from their mothers. There is no mother cat here, so how could these two kittens be real?"

But Lone only ordered, "Take it away."

The next day, as Everett Lone was telling his story to a friend, he was interrupted by a noise among the picture frames on his mantle. It was another kitten, and it knocked the clock onto the floor.

Again Lone instructed his servant, "Take it away!"
Only this time he added "At once!" Then Lone and his
friend sat down and sent a rather nasty note to Richard Evans, telling him in no uncertain terms what they
thought of him.

When Richard Evans received it, he didn't understand. He went to the marketplace of the city and found
Dana Da looking pale and exhausted. And he read him
the letter.

Da laughed. "You see? That is my sending. I told
you it would work. Give me another ten rupees, if you
please."

"But Da, what does it mean?"

"It means cats . . . cats . . . cats! And more cats! I will
send a hundred cats! No, a thousand cats! Ten thousand! This sending will make me famous!"

But he looked ill, and Evans wondered if he would
live to experience such greatness.

On one point, however, it appeared that Dana Da
was right. When a man who hates cats opens a drawer
and discovers one among his socks, finds one sticking
its head out of his pajama pocket or above the rim of
his boot, hears a telltale "Meow" from under his chair
during dinner, then wakes up one morning with a

kitten on his chest—and above all when there's no logi-cal explanation—it's enough to get on his nerves.

Everett Lone's eyes grew red from lack of sleep. His voice went up half an octave, and every little noise made him jump. He was not having fun.

At the same time, another player entered the story.

This was the local wizard, who was furious to hear that someone else was successfully practicing his same business in his territory. Afraid that his custom-ers would begin to go to this newcomer for their ser-vices, he began to tell them that it was *he*, not Dana Da, who was responsible for the sending that everyone had now heard of (thanks to a word dropped by Everett Lone's servant).

The wizard wrote a letter to Dana Da claiming all the credit for himself. After Richard Evans read it to him, Da looked furious for a moment, but then he laughed, although the laughing clearly tired him.

"So," he said, "that is the old man's game, is it? Then the time has come. Write what I tell you, but first give me ten more rupees, please." And he dictated a letter to the old wizard and his followers, openly challenging him. It ended, "And if this is your work, let the sending go on, but if it be mine, let it stop in two more days. On that day, there will be 12 kittens. Twelve! And then no more. Let the people judge between us." He asked Richard Evans to have it read aloud in the marketplace by a scribe. Then everyone waited.

On the specified day, it seemed that half the English population of the city "happened to drop by" Everett Lone's home. Clearly they were curious. Sure enough, kittens began to appear first thing in the morning, and continued throughout the day, and none of the English gentry could believe it. Three kittens showed up in the bathrooms, two were found playing on the rug in front of the hearth, and the others turned up in all sorts of odd places.

"I say, Lone, what's that behind that potted plant?"

"Look what I found in your entry hall as I was coming in, old man!"

And later, conclusively, "Good heavens! There's a kitten in my teacup!"

This was the last straw. There is nothing more sacred to an English person than a cup of tea. The very idea of a kitten appearing there was the ultimate horror.

Appropriately enough, that was the twelfth cat, and then the rain of kittens stopped.

Well, of course, it was just as Dana Da had predicted in his letter. The old wizard was disgraced, while Everett Lone, who could stand it no longer, packed up and left town.

However, Dana Da himself was rapidly headed on an even longer journey. He lay dying in the spare bedroom of Richard Evans' home, where Evans had brought him in his concern.

Da had little energy to celebrate his great victory. "The sending is done," he whispered to Evans. "But the effort has killed me."

Richard Evans, who genuinely liked him, smiled. "Nonsense," he said. "I am afraid you are dying, but the rest is simply not true. Tell me honestly now, how did you do it?"

As Richard Evans bent low, Da whispered, "You gave me ten rupees several times, and each time I simply paid Lone's servant two for placing cats, little cats, all over his house. There are no more cats left in the marketplace."

Dana Da laughed at his own words. Then he closed his eyes and disappeared in a way that was no mere illusion.

Afterwards, Richard Evans never told the secret. Dana Da's reputation never suffered, and Everett Lone never returned.

And in the years that followed, whenever Richard Evans would think back, he always found himself smiling at the sheer, gorgeous simplicity behind ...

The Sending of Dana Da.

For such a brightly lit place, your local library or bookstore contains many spooky corners—within the pages of books, you understand! There you can find more wondrous stories from Oscar Wilde, Nathaniel Hawthorne, Rudyard Kipling, and other authors. And you won't stand a ghost of a chance of ever running out!

PART II:
THREE SPOOKY PLAYS

The Canterville Ghost

Dramatized by Chris Bauer

After the original performance by Jim Weiss

You are about to put on a play called "The Canterville Ghost." It is based on Jim Weiss's version of the story. But you don't have to do it in exactly the same way it was read! The fun of plays is that the same story can be told in many different ways. You get to bring your own imagination and tell this story your own way.

Below you will find some suggestions about how to put the play on, but they are only suggestions. Use your imagination and add your own ideas to this play whenever you think it would make it more fun for you to perform, or for your audience to watch!

Cast

First, you need a "Cast." The Cast are the people who play the different characters. If you have a lot of actors in your Cast, each actor can be one character. If you don't have as many actors, one actor can play several characters.

Usually if an actor is playing several characters, those are characters that don't have as much to do in the play. For example, in this play, whoever played Sir Simon de Canterville wouldn't be any other characters since Sir Simon is already in the play a lot. But the same person who played Washington could also play the Duke of Cheshire, since those two characters are not in the play as much.

Depending on who you have as actors, you can do "gender-blind" casting. This means that boys can play girls' parts and girls can play boys' parts. A lot of theaters do this when they have a role that was written specifically for a man or woman, but one is not available.

The Narrator can be a boy or a girl.

List of Characters

Narrator
Sir Simon de Canterville
Mr. Otis
Mrs. Otis
Virginia
Washington
Stars (Twin One)
Stripes (Twin Two)
Lord Canterville
Mrs. Umney

Costumes and Props

You should try to find some clothes that look like they could be from the middle to late 1800s in England, because that is when the story is set. You can do some research in books or on the internet to see what people dressed like back then. Remember, the Otis family is American so they might dress differently than Lord Canterville or Mrs.

Umney. Also remember that Sir Simon is a ghost from the Middle Ages, so he will also dress differently than the others.

The Narrator does not have to have a costume, but he or she can, if you would like.

"Props" are anything the characters use. These are the props you will need:

1. Pinkerton's Stain Remover. You can use an old lipstick case, or even just an eraser.
2. Doctor Dobell's Miracle Cure. You can use any little glass bottle.
3. Teacups
4. Sir Simon's diary. Any big heavy book will do.
5. The Otis Ghost. You can make the Otis Ghost from a broom, a white sheet, and if you want you can even make a face for him out of a turnip or some other white vegetable! Also, don't forget the cardboard sign which reads "Ye Otis Ghost, Ye Only True and Original Spooke. Beware of Ye Imitations."
6. Jewels. You can use costume jewels, beads, or even just a box with JEWELS written on it.

If you're missing any props or costumes, you can just mime. Miming is when you move your hands like you're holding or using something, but there's nothing actually there.

For example, you might not have a bathrobe and slippers for Mr. Otis. When you get to the part where it says Mr. Otis puts on a bathrobe and slippers, the actor playing Mr. Otis can just pretend to put on a bathrobe and slippers.

Set

The "Set" of a play is where it takes place, its "setting." This play takes place in and around Canterville Chase. You can do it anywhere in your house. Try to make it look like an old English home if you want to. You can hang blankets from the walls to be "tapestries," or add anything else you think might make your house look more like Canterville Chase—old-looking chairs and side tables, candlesticks, etc.

Sound

All sounds can be made by the actors who are not on stage at that point.

There should be somewhere, out of sight, that actors can be when they are not on stage. In the theater this is called being "Backstage." The sounds can be made from Backstage.

The Play

When you perform the play, you will see each character's name followed by a colon, like this:

SIR SIMON DE CANTERVILLE:

After the colon will be some words. These are the character's lines. When you play that character, say whatever comes after the colon. So if you saw this;

SIR SIMON DE CANTERVILLE: Boo!

and you were playing Sir Simon, you would say "Boo!"

If you see more than one character's names, for example the twins Stars and Stripes, like this:

STARS and STRIPES:
it means both characters say the line at the same time.

One more thing; if you see something in parentheses after the name, it's an instruction that tells you how the line should be read. For example,

SIR SIMON DE CANTERVILLE: (Angrily)
that means that whatever he says, he should say ANGRILY!

If you want to memorize your lines and perform it that way, that's great! If you want to read them off the paper, that's absolutely fine, too.

Staging

There are some theater terms you should know.

The most important ones are "Stage Left," "Stage Right," and "Center Stage." If the play says a character should stand Stage Left, it means that if you are playing that character and you are standing and facing your audience, you should be to the left of the stage. The reason it's called "Stage Left" is that for the audience, who is facing you, it's the right! It can be a little confusing, but just remember, when you are facing the audience, Stage Left is *your* left and Stage Right is *your* right. Center Stage means, very simply, that you move to the center of the stage.

It's also important to remember that you don't have to be on an actual stage to use these terms. If you're doing a play in your living room, you can still say you are "Stage Left" or "Stage Right" or "Center Stage," depending on where you stand in the space you are using to perform.

Another term you should know is "Stage Directions." In the play, you will see some sentences in parentheses. These are your Stage Directions. They tell you where the characters should be standing, and sometimes what they should be doing.

Finally, you will see some Stage Directions that say "Lights Up" or "Lights Down." This means, simply, that you turn the lights on or off to begin and end your play.

One last thing

Remember, the most important part of this play is that you have fun! If you don't have all the props, or if somebody stands someplace different from where the instructions say, or if you decide you want to change everything and do it your own way, all those things are not only fine, they are wonderful! Mistakes in theater can be the most fun part of the whole show as long as you just keep going along and enjoying yourself.

The Canterville Ghost

(Lights Up. Narrator enters, stands Stage Left.)

NARRATOR: Everyone told Hiram Otis that he was making the mistake of his life when he decided to move his family to Canterville Chase. Even Lord Canterville tried to tell him about it.

(Lord Canterville and Mr. Otis enter, stand Center Stage.)

LORD CANTERVILLE: You see, it's been some years since we Cantervilles have lived at the old place ourselves. We stuck it out for generations, centuries in fact, ever since the ghost of my ancestor, Sir Simon de Canterville, first appeared. What finally cut it for us was the evening my grand-aunt felt two skeletal hands on her shoulders as she was dressing for dinner!

MR. OTIS: We'll take the place and everything in it, including the furniture and the servants. I don't wish to sound rude, my lord, but I represent a modern nation. We don't believe in any superstitious mumbo-jumbo we can't understand, except maybe for Congress. We'll take our chances with this ghost business.

(Lord Canterville exits, and the Otis family enters and stands Stage Right: Mrs. Otis, Virginia, Stars, Stripes, and Washington. If you don't have enough actors for all of them and some actors have to play different members of the Otis family, they can come out one at a time and then run off stage and switch characters.)

MRS. OTIS: You found us a place that's haunted? Hiram, how charming!

STARS and STRIPES: We're going to live in a castle?

STARS, STRIPES, and WASHINGTON: (Enthusiastically) Hooray! Wooh! Yeah!

(Stars, Stripes, and Washington should all jump around and make lots of very excited noises. Then they all start walking across the stage towards the Narrator. While the Narrator talks they should walk all the way towards him or her and then turn around and walk back to Stage Right like they are going to Canterville Chase.)

NARRATOR: When the Otis family arrived at Canterville Chase they found the housekeeper, Mrs. Umney, waiting on the wide front steps.

(Mrs. Umney enters and stands Stage Right, waiting for the Otis family.)

MRS. UMNEY: I bid you welcome to your new home at Canterville Chase.

(Otis family follows Mrs. Umney to Center Stage and they all sit down. Mrs. Umney brings them teacups.)

NARRATOR: The Otises were soon seated in the wood-paneled library, sipping tea before a low fire. Mrs. Otis noticed a dull red stain on the floor by the fireplace.

MRS. OTIS: Mrs. Umney, it seems something has been spilled there. Would you be kind enough to see to it?

MRS. UMNEY: Oh madam, I'm afraid that what's been spilt there cannot be removed so easily as all that. It's blood. It was on this very spot that Sir Simon de Canterville murdered his wife, the Lady Eleanore, many centuries ago. He himself disappeared a few years later, and was never seen again. Or at least . . . he was never seen alive. His guilty spirit still haunts this estate. And as for the bloodstain, well, it's been removed before, but it always returns.

WASHINGTON: Nonsense! Whoever dealt with this stain before didn't have all the modern conveniences! We'll just take it out with a little bit of Pinkerton's Champion Stain Remover!

(Washington gets on the floor and rubs out the stain with his Pinkerton's Champion Stain Remover.)

WASHINGTON: There! All gone! Pinkerton's always does the trick, no matter how old the stain may be!

(All characters freeze motionless during the Narrator's next speech.)

NARRATOR: The next morning, however, they found the bloodstain back on the library floor.

WASHINGTON: (Confused) That's funny. Pinkerton's has always worked perfectly.

(He rubs the stain out again, and keeps rubbing as the Narrator talks.)

NARRATOR: He rubbed out the stain again, but it was back the next day, and no matter how often he removed it, it was back the next day and the next, even when Mr. Otis took to locking the library door at night.

(Everyone leaves the stage except Mr. and Mrs. Otis, who lie down Center Stage.)

NARRATOR: And then, late one night, hours after the family had fallen asleep in their large four-poster beds, Mr. Otis awoke quite suddenly to a loud metallic clanking in the corridor.

(Everyone off stage makes rattling noises with pennies in a can, metal dog leashes, or anything you have that can rattle like chains. Mr. Otis gets up.)

NARRATOR: He sat up, quietly donned his slippers and robe so as not to awaken his wife, drew a small bottle from his dresser drawer, and opened the bedroom door.

(Sir Simon enters and stands Stage Right.)

NARRATOR: Then he stopped in his tracks, for not five feet away from him, lit eerily by moonlight through the hall window, was a horrible vision!

(Sir Simon takes a few steps towards Mr. Otis, in as scary a way as he can.)

MR. OTIS: My dear sir, if you are going to move through our home wearing those chains I must insist that you oil them. We need our sleep, especially the children. Therefore, I have taken the liberty of bringing you this little bottle of Tammany Rising Sun Metal Lubricator, made in the U.S. of A. Just a small amount properly applied should do the trick. Thank you and good evening.

(Mr. Otis exits. Sir Simon walks to Center Stage and looks around. He is confused and upset. He throws away the bottle. Stars and Stripes enter and stand Stage Right. Sir Simon sees them and prepares to be his scariest.)

SIR SIMON: (Scarily and loudly) Ha. . . . hahahaha . . . AHAHAHAHAHAHAHAHAHAHAHAHAHAAAAA!

(The twins don't look scared at all. Mrs. Otis enters and stands with the twins Stage Right.)

MRS. OTIS: My goodness, you don't sound at all well. If you'll just give me a moment I can offer you some of Doctor Dobell's Miracle Cure, which is absolutely the thing for stomach ailments or influenza.

(Sir Simon looks very upset. Mrs. Otis and the twins exit, and Sir Simon runs back and forth across the stage while the Narrator talks.)

NARRATOR: The Canterville Ghost thrust himself hurriedly through the walls of the old house and reappeared at last in a concealed chamber far from the Otises' bedrooms. Throwing himself into a chair, which could be seen right through him, he sat catching his breath.

(Sir Simon gets his diary and sits down.)

SIR SIMON: What is this world coming to? Why, in over three centuries of haunting I have never been so insulted, so ill used, so ignored!

NARRATOR: To reassure himself of his longstanding skills, he lifted up his diary, a large volume with a dark leather cover. He opened to one of his favorite entries.

SIR SIMON: (Reading from the diary) This evening I had a most gratifying encounter with Reverend Dampier, the local clergyman, who had had the temerity to doubt my existence. Well after tonight he will doubt no more! As he left the castle library, I followed him into the hallway and blew out his candle, and then each time he lit it again I extinguished it again until he ran through the darkened halls screaming and bumping into the furniture in such fear that I had to stop pursuing him because I was laughing too hard.

(Sir Simon closes the book and stands up.)

SIR SIMON: Why, I am absolutely at the top of my profession. In all this part of England there is no ghostly spirit half so versatile or with half my reputation.

NARRATOR: The next few days passed quietly enough, but this was merely the lull before the storm. In the past, the mere appearance of the Canterville Ghost had been enough to frighten anyone. These newcomers were a different sort altogether, and the ghost had determined to meet the challenge. He was only taking his time, carefully planning a grand and truly terrifying appearance.

SIR SIMON: This will send them hurrying back to the colonies on the next ship! I have settled upon the combination of Bloody

Hans, the Butcher of Hamburg, with the always effective Desolate Prince. I will appear as a green, icy cold corpse dressed in old bloody clothing which I shall unwind with one hand. And then my supreme moment; having removed the bloody grave cloths I stand revealed in the form of . . . a skeleton! With bleached white bones . . . and, I think . . . yes, just one rolling eyeball. And now, to practice. Ahem. Ooooooh! Ooooooooooh! Hmm, perhaps in a higher key . . . ooooooooooh!"

NARRATOR: And so, having laid his plans, he waited until the great old clock in the upstairs hall struck midnight. Then the Canterville Ghost left his place in the shadows to strike terror into the hearts of the unsuspecting Otis family. Silently he stole through the hallway towards Washington's room. He turned the corner . . . and let out a terrible wail of terror, leaping backwards, for there in front of him was a dreadful sight!

(Stars and Stripes run out carrying the Otis ghost. They chase Sir Simon all over the stage with it. He keeps running away, looking very scared.)

NARRATOR: Seized with panic, he flung himself up the chimney and back to his secret room. Once there he threw himself down, gasping for breath.

(The twins exit, leaving the Otis ghost Stage Right. Sir Simon sits Center Stage. He is very scared, but he manages to calm down.)

SIR SIMON: This is my haunting place. I am not about to surrender it to some Johnny-come-lately spirit. Besides, if I can convince the other ghost to join forces with me, together we might frighten away these Otises at last.

(Sir Simon goes to Stage Right and finds the Otis Ghost. He stands there and looks at it, then turns around and sadly goes back to Center Stage. He lies down on the floor and curls up into a ball.)

NARRATOR: Something went out of the Canterville Ghost. Slowly he dragged his way back to his room, slumped, and sat unmoving. The next day he decided that he would no longer replenish the bloodstain on the library floor. He did determine to resume his activities several weeks later when Virginia Otis's young suitor, the Duke of Cheshire, came to visit from his own nearby estate. In the end, however, picturing the Otis twins lying in wait, the ghost couldn't quite summon up the necessary resolve. And so the adoring young Duke was able to spend time with Virginia undisturbed.

(Duke of Cheshire and Virginia enter Stage Right.)

NARRATOR: On their horseback ride over the estate, Virginia tore her riding jacket on a branch and they rode back to the house.

VIRGINIA: Edward, I'll just run up and change my outfit.

(Duke exits, Virginia walks to Center Stage and sees the ghost all curled up.)

VIRGINIA: I'm very sorry for all the trouble, but if you'll just be patient a few more days my brothers and I will be going off to school. Then, if you'll behave yourself, no one will bother you.

(Sir Simon sits up.)

SIR SIMON: Well, really, it's no good asking me to "behave" myself. It is my job to moan and rattle chains and all the rest that goes with it. If I cannot do these things I've simply no reason to exist. But thank you for your concern.

VIRGINIA: It's just common decency. Really, I'm quite annoyed with you. You had no right to steal my paints from my paint box to refurbish your dreadful bloodstain. Besides, Mrs. Umney told us the day we arrived that you had killed your wife.

SIR SIMON: Perfectly true. It was an accident, of course. I had loved her, you know. I took to wandering the estate at all hours of the day and night, and when, a few years later, I too crossed over—

VIRGINIA: When you died, you mean?

SIR SIMON: Well ... there's the problem you see. I never died, quite. I had experienced such guilt that instead of finding eternal peace I was condemned to walk these halls forever.

VIRGINIA: Is there no hope for you? Yes, there must always be hope.

(Sir Simon stands up.)

SIR SIMON: Perhaps you could open the doorway for me. I have seen you during these weeks. Love is always with you, and love is stronger than death itself. You, child, who are so filled with compassion for others, you who have boundless faith, faith enough even to believe that an old accursed spirit such as I might yet be saved ... you might hold a vision of hope for me still. And if you weep, and if you pray, perhaps I too will remember how, and the angel of death might have mercy on me. Oh, but you will see fearful shapes and visions in the darkness, and hear terrifying voices warning you to abandon your hope. There are always such voices in the world, Virginia. But if you are brave and persist, they cannot harm you, for they've no real power over the faith of a loving heart.

VIRGINIA: Let us try.

(Sir Simon and Virginia turn and walk offstage. Everyone offstage should make scary noises, moaning, wailing, like lots and lots of ghosts. The Otis family and the Duke enter and stand Center Stage.)

NARRATOR: About ten minutes later, the silence was broken by a bell ringing through the house, summoning the Otis family to afternoon tea. Their guest, the Duke of Cheshire, was disturbed when Virginia did not appear with the others, but not until dinnertime did they feel real alarm.

(The Otises and the Duke start running around, calling to Virginia and looking for her.)

NARRATOR: Mr. Otis had just declared he would call in the police when the old upstairs clock began to chime midnight. As its last stroke ended, they heard a dreadful cry, and then beautiful, unearthly music began to fill the old house. A panel at the top of the staircase slid back, and there stood Virginia.

VIRGINIA: I'm so sorry to have worried you. I was with Sir Simon.

OTIS FAMILY and DUKE: What!

VIRGINIA: Yes. I had a long talk with him. He lived quite a wicked life, I'm afraid, and he felt so badly about it afterward that he couldn't sleep for the longest time. He asked me if I could help him, and I did. And now at last he can rest. She has forgiven him. And look, before he died he gave me this box of beautiful jewels to keep!

(Virginia shows everyone the jewels, then hands them to Mr. Otis. Everyone but Mr. Otis exits. Lord Canterville enters, and the two of them stands Center Stage.)

NARRATOR: Well, there's little more to tell, but what there is is worth telling. Mr. Otis insisted that Lord Canterville receive back the magnificent jewels the ghost had given to Virginia.

MR. OTIS: These are Canterville jewels, after all.

LORD CANTERVILLE: My dear sir, if you'll recall, when you acquired Canterville Chase you acquired everything in it. These are quite properly yours, and from what you tell me the young lady certainly earned them. Besides, the old fellow . . . you know whom I mean . . . gave them to her himself. I suspect that if I was so rash as to receive them from you he'd be out of his grave and paying me rather a nasty visit before the week was out. No, I insist they stay with your daughter.

(Mr. Otis and Lord Canterville exit, Virginia and the Duke enter and stand Center Stage.)

NARRATOR: And so they did, although it was some years before she had the opportunity to wear them. On that memorable occasion, both she and her jewels were the subject of profound admiration as the young lady was presented at court to good Queen Victoria herself.

DUKE: Your Majesty, may I have the pleasure of presenting to you Virginia, my wife.

(Lights Down, then Lights Up again so everybody can come out and bow while the audience claps, because they are very impressed at the play you have just done.)

Dr. Heidegger's Experiment

Dramatized by Chris Bauer

After the original performance by Jim Weiss

You are about to put on a play called "Dr. Heidegger's Experiment." It is based on Jim Weiss's version of the story. But you don't have to do it in exactly the same way it was read! The fun of plays is that the same story can be told in many different ways. You get to bring your own imagination and tell this story your own way.

Below you will find some suggestions about how to put the play on, but they are only just suggestions to make it easier for you. You should use your imagination and add your own ideas to this play whenever you think it would make it more fun for you to perform or for your audience to watch!

Cast

First, you need a "Cast." The Cast are the people who play the different characters. Unlike some other plays, you can't have people playing more than one role, since all five actors are onstage the whole time.

Depending on who you have as actors, you can do "gender-blind" casting. This means that boys can play girls' parts and girls can play boys' parts. A lot of theaters do this when they have a role that was written specifically for a man or woman, but one is not available.

List of Characters

Dr. Heidegger
Mr. Medbourne
Colonel Killigrew
Mr. Gascoigne
Widow Wycherly

Costumes and Props

You should try to find some clothes that look like they could be from America in the 1830s, because that is when the story is set. You can do some research in books or on the internet to see what people dressed like back then.

"Props" are anything the characters use. These are the props you will need:

1. Leather book
2. Pressed rose (you can cut one out of paper if you don't have a real one)
3. Vase full of water (use a PLASTIC vase, because it gets knocked over and we don't want it to break and hurt anybody!)
4. Four champagne glasses (regular cups are OK too)
5. Paper and pencil (whoever plays Mr. Medbourne should have these in his pocket)
6. Full red rose. To change the shriveled rose into a full red rose, you could try having two vases of water, one with a red rose already in it. When it comes time for the brown rose to change into a red one, you can cover the vase with a cloth, put it on the ground behind the table, put the cloth over the vase with

the red rose in it, bring it back up to the table, and then take the cloth away. If you can think of a more clever way to do it, then go for it!

Any props or costumes you don't have, you can just mime. Miming is when you move your hands like you're holding or using something, but there's actually nothing there.

Set

The "Set" of a play is where it takes place, its "setting." This play takes place in Dr. Heidegger's house. You can do it anywhere in your house. This is a very easy set because all you need is a table and some chairs. But you can do anything else you can think of to make your house look like what you think Dr. Heidegger's house would look like. If you want to, you can do some research and find out what houses in America looked like in the 1830s.

One thing you especially need is a picture of Sylvia somewhere on the wall. This can be a portrait or a picture of a woman in old-fashioned clothing, or even something you draw.

Sound

Sounds should be made by helpers who are not onstage and are hidden from the audience, but are close enough to be heard.

The Play

When you perform the play, you will see each character's name followed by a colon, like this:

DR HEIDEGGER:

After the colon will be some words. These are the character's lines. When you play that character, you say whatever comes after the colon. So if you saw this;

DR HEIDEGGER: The Fountain of Youth.

and you were playing Dr. Heidegger, you would say "The Fountain of Youth."

If you see more than one character's names, like this:

COLONEL KILLIGREW and WIDOW WYCHERLY:

it means both characters say the line at the same time.

One more thing; if you see something in parentheses after the name, it's an instruction that tells you how the line should be read. For example,

DR HEIDEGGER: (Angrily)

that means that whatever he says, he should say ANGRILY!

If you want to memorize your lines and perform it that way, that's great! If you want to read them off the paper, that's fine, too.

Staging

There are some theater terms you should know.

The most important ones are "Stage Left," "Stage Right," and "Center Stage." If the play says a character should stand Stage Left, it means that if you are playing that character and you are standing and facing your audience, you should be to the left of the stage. The reason it's called "Stage Left" is that for the audience, who is facing you, it's the right! It can be a little confusing, but just remember, when you are facing the audience, Stage Left is *your* left and Stage Right is *your* right. Center Stage means, very simply, that you move to the center of the stage.

It's also important to remember that you don't have to be on an actual stage to use these terms. If you're doing a play in your living room, you can still say you are "Stage Left" or "Stage Right" or "Center Stage" depending on where you stand in the space you are using to perform.

Another term you should know is "Stage Directions." In the play, you will see some sentences in parentheses. These are your Stage Directions. They tell you where the characters should be standing, and sometimes what they should be doing.

Finally, you will see some Stage Directions that say "Lights Up" or "Lights Down." This means, simply, that you turn the lights on or off to begin and end your play.

Physical Acting

Dr. Heidegger's experiment is a special play because it lets you explore **acting physically.**

When we act, we do a lot of it with our **voices** and our **facial expressions**. In this story, four old people grow younger and younger, and then suddenly grow old again. You will have to show this happening by using your bodies.

In the beginning you are old; when you drink the water, you grow younger. Watch older people, and look carefully at how they move. You should copy their movements when you play the older versions of the characters, and then as your characters get younger you can move more freely. Think of it like this; you start the play as your grandparents, then you become your parents, then you become you, and finally you become your grandparents again! So watch how your parents and grandparents move, and see if you can move and use your body differently for each age you are playing.

There is also a fight in this play, where three of the characters start fighting and knock over a vase.

When you fight on stage, it is very important that you not *actually* wrestle or punch. You have to make it *look* like you are fighting, but the most important thing is that everybody is in control all the time. Practice the fight several times and make sure you do it exactly the same way every time. Do *not* do anything that might get somebody hurt! You don't have to throw each other into things or knock each other on the ground. Instead, grab each other's shoulders and lean back and forth, then bump into the table so the vase falls off. BE CAREFUL. DO NOT HURT EACH OTHER!

One Last Thing

Remember, the most important part of this play is that you have fun!

If you don't have all the props, or if somebody stands someplace different from where the instructions say, or if you decide you want to change everything and do it your own way, all those things are not only fine, they are wonderful! Mistakes in theater can be the most fun part of the whole show as long as you just keep going along and enjoying yourself.

Dr. Heidegger's Experiment

(Lights up. Mr. Medbourne, Colonel Killigrew, Mr. Gascoigne, and Widow Wycherly are sitting around a table Center Stage. Dr. Heidegger is standing next to them.)

DR. HEIDEGGER: My dear old friends, I've asked you here today in hope that you will assist me in one of those little experiments with which I amuse myself here in my study. I have something to show you.

(Dr. Heidegger puts the vase on the table, then gets the leather book and takes out the dead brown rose.)

DR. HEIDEGGER: (Sadly) This rose blossomed 55 years ago. It was given to me by Sylvia, whose portrait hangs there.

(Dr. Heidegger points to the picture of Sylvia.)

DR. HEIDEGGER: For 55 years it has rested between the pages of this book. Now looking at it, would you think it possible that this rose should ever bloom again?

WIDOW WYCHERLY: Nonsense. You might as well ask if an old woman's wrinkled face could bloom again.

DR. HEIDEGGER: Look.

(Dr. Heidegger drops the rose into the vase. See the "Props" section for a suggestion about how to switch out the rose.)

ALL THE GUESTS: Marvelous! How did you do it?

DR. HEIDEGGER: Have you ever heard of the Fountain of Youth, which Ponce de Leon, the Spanish explorer, searched for two or three centuries ago?

MR. MEDBOURNE: But did Ponce de Leon ever find it?

DR. HEIDEGGER: No, for he looked in the wrong place. I'm told it lies in Southern Florida, not far from Lake Macaco. By its springs are century-old trees which, drinking its waters, never grow old. Through a roundabout set of events, this vase has come to me, full of the waters of the Fountain of Youth.

COLONEL KILLIGREW: Very useful for a flower, Doctor, but tell me, how would this liquid affect a human being?

DR. HEIDEGGER: You shall judge for yourself, Colonel. All of you shall judge for yourselves. You are welcome to as much of this wondrous water as you need in order to restore to you the bloom of youth. As for me, having encountered so much trouble growing old I'm in no hurry to grow young again. With your permission I'll simply observe the progress of the experiment.

(Dr. Heidegger fills four champagne glasses with water from the vase, and the other four all reach for them.)

DR. HEIDEGGER: Wait! Before you drink, my respectable old friends, consider for a moment the lives you have lived. With all this experience, wouldn't it be fitting to write up some general rules for your guidance in navigating, for a second time, through the perils of youth? Why waste the wisdom of a lifetime? You could live a wise and virtuous life, and set a fine example for other young people.

(The other four all laugh at Dr. Heidegger.)

MR. MEDBOURNE: Why, we should hardly need a list of reminders, Doctor. Surely we would know better this time!

DR. HEIDEGGER: Very well, then. Drink.

(The four friends all drink, and they feel a change. Try to show they feel a change by shifting in your chair, changing the expression on your face.)

WIDOW WYCHERLY: Give us more!

MR. GASCOIGNE, COLONEL KILLIGREW, and MR. MEDBOURNE: Yes, we are younger, but we are still too old! Give us more, hurry!

DR. HEIDEGGER: Patience, it has taken you a long time to grow old. Surely you can wait half an hour to grow young.

(The four guests all moan, whine, maybe slam their heads down on the table.)

DR. HEIDEGGER: Very well, then. The water is at your service.

(Dr. Heidegger refills the glasses, the other four drink them. They all feel even younger, and all look at each other.)

COLONEL KILLIGREW: My dear Widow! You are absolutely charming!

(Widow Wycherly gets up and runs to look at herself in a mirror Stage Right. You don't have to have an actual mirror, but she should act like she is looking in one. Meanwhile, Mr. Medbourne takes out a paper and pencil and starts writing, Colonel Killigrew gets up and starts dancing around Stage Left, and Mr. Gascoigne talks. Meanwhile, Dr. Heidegger refills all the glasses and puts the vase down right at the edge of the table. This is so the others can "accidentally" knock it off in the next part.)

MR. GASCOIGNE: I tell you Medbourne, it's not too late as long as there are true patriots about, men and women who are unashamed of their devotion to the flag! Now what this country needs—

(Colonel Killigrew cuts him off.)

COLONEL KILLIGREW: (Singing) He floats through the air with the greatest of ease, the daring young man on the flying trapeze!

WIDOW WYCHERLY: My dear old Doctor, let's have another glass!

DR. HEIDEGGER: Certainly, my dear madam. You see, I have already filled the glasses!

(They all drink again, and then they all start jumping and dancing around the room except for the Doctor.)

ALL BUT DOCTOR: We are young! We are young!

WIDOW WYCHERLY: Doctor, you dear old soul! Get up and dance with me!

DR. HEIDEGGER: Pray excuse me, I am old, and my dancing days are long gone. But I am sure any of these young gentlemen would be delighted to dance with so lovely a partner.

COLONEL KILLIGREW: Yes, dance with me, Clara!

MR. GASCOIGNE: No, no, she shall dance with me!

MR. MEDBOURNE: She promised me her hand fifty years ago!

(They all try to dance with Widow Wycherly, but end up fighting with each other instead Stage Right, next to the table. Check the notes in the Physical Action section of the Instructions about how to do the fight correctly. They end up knocking over the table, and the vase falls, spilling the water.)

DR. HEIDEGGER: Come, come, gentlemen. And you too, lady. Look what you have done! My dear Sylvia's rose . . . it appears to be fading again.

(Dr. Heidegger picks up the rose and switches it with the brown rose in the vase hidden behind the table. He sits down. The other four guests shiver, and then grow old again. The actors should stop dancing around, and change their bodies back into the positions they had when they were old, more bent over, moving slowly, etc.)

MR. MEDBOURNE: No! No!

MR. GASCOIGNE: Not so soon!

WIDOW WYCHERLY: Am I . . . are we old again?

DR. HEIDEGGER: Yes. Yes, you are old again. And the water of youth is gone. And as for me, I am not sorry. If the Fountain itself gushed by my doorstep I would not bathe in it. Such is the lesson you have taught me.

(The other four all exit Stage Left, talking about how they are going to go find the Fountain of Youth. The actors can make up the lines here, things like "Let's book train tickets to Florida!" and "I can't wait!" Dr. Heidegger puts the brown rose back in the book, closes it, then sits in his chair. Lights Down, then Lights Up again so you can all bow.)

The Sending of Dana Da

Dramatized by Chris Bauer
After the original performance by Jim Weiss

You are about to put on a play called "The Sending of Dana Da." It is based on Jim Weiss's version of the story. But you don't have to do it in exactly the same way it was read! The fun of plays is that the same story can be told in many different ways. You get to bring your own imagination and tell this story your own way.

Below you will find some suggestions about how to put the play on, but they are *only* suggestions. You should use your imagination and add your own ideas to this play, whenever you think it would make it more fun for you to perform or for your audience to watch!

Cast

First you need a "Cast." The Cast are the people who play the different characters. If you have a lot of actors in your Cast, each actor can be one character. If you don't have as many actors, one actor can play several characters. Usually if an actor is playing several characters, they are characters who don't have as much to do in the play.

Depending on who you have as actors, you can do "gender-blind" casting. This means that boys can play girls' parts and girls can play boys' parts. A lot of theaters do this when they have a role that was written specifically for a man or woman, but one is not available.

The Narrator can be a boy or a girl.

List of Characters

Narrator
Dana Da
Richard Evans
Everett Lone
Lone's servant
Everett's guests (2 to 3 people)

Costumes and Props

You should try to find some clothes that look like they could be from the 1890s. Some of the characters are from England, and some are from India. You can do some research in books or on the internet to see what people dressed like back then. The Narrator does not have to have a costume, but he or she can if you would like.

"Props" are anything the characters use. These are the props you will need:

1. Money (you can just use paper you cut up into rectangular pieces)
2. A rug (small enough to carry)
3. Food (for Richard and Dana's meal)
4. Letter
5. Book
6. Cats!

The Sending of Dana Da is about a "curse" that is cast on Everett Lone, and it causes him to find cats in his house. You can use stuffed animals, or you can cut cats out of paper. Before the show starts, you should hide the cats around the stage, and even under and around the seats of your audience, so that when you reach the point in the play where the guests are finding cats you can run around and "find" all the cats hidden everywhere! There should be one on Everett Lone's bed and one behind his chair, but other than that, use your imagination and hide them everywhere

Any props or costumes you don't have, you can just mime. Miming is when you move your hands like you're holding or using something, but there's actually nothing there.

Set

The "Set" of a play is where it takes place, its "setting."

This play takes place in the homes of Richard Evans and Everett Lone. You should make Stage Left the home of Richard Evans and Stage Right the home of Everett Lone. If you don't know what that means, look in the section of the Introduction that talks about theater terms.

Richard Evans' home should have a table and two chairs in it, and Everett Lone's home should have a chair and a "bed." (You don't need an actual bed, you can just use another chair or a blanket on the floor or anything like that.)

Sound

All sounds can be made by the actors who are not on stage right now! There should be somewhere out of sight that the actors can be when they are not on stage. In the theater this is called being "Backstage." Backstage should be in a place where the audience can hear, but not see, the actors.

The Play

When you perform the play, you will see each character's name followed by a colon, like this:

DANA DA:

After the colon will be some words. These are the character's lines. When you play that character, you say whatever comes after the colon. So if you saw this;

DANA DA: Cats!
and you were playing Dana Da, you would say "Cats!"

If you see more than one character's names like this:

GUEST 1 and GUEST 2: Oh my!
it means both characters say the line at the same time.

One more thing; if you see something in parentheses after the name, it's an instruction that tells you how the line should be read. For example,

EVERETT LONE: (Angrily)
that means that whatever he says, he should say ANGRILY!

If you want to memorize your lines and perform it that way, that's great! If you want to read them off the paper, that's perfectly fine too.

There are some theater terms you should know.

The most important ones are "Stage Left," "Stage Right," and "Center Stage." If the play says a character should stand Stage Left, it means that if you are playing that character and you are standing and facing your audience, you should be to the left of the stage. The reason it's called "Stage Left" is that for the audience, who is facing you, it's the right! It can be a little confusing, but just remember, when you are facing the audience, Stage Left is *your* left and Stage Right is *your* right. Center Stage means, very simply, that you move to the center of the stage.

It's also important to remember that you don't have to be on an actual stage to use these terms. If you're doing a play in your living room, you can still say you are "Stage Left" or "Stage Right" or "Center Stage" depending on where you stand in the space you are using to perform.

Another term you should know is "Stage Directions." In the play, you will see some sentences in parentheses. These are your Stage Directions. They tell you where the characters should be standing, and sometimes what they should be doing.

Finally, you will see some Stage Directions that say "Lights Up" or "Lights Down." This means, simply, that you turn the lights on or off to begin and end your play.

One Last Thing

Remember, the most important part of this play is that you have fun! If you don't have all the props, or if somebody stands someplace different from where the instructions say, or if you decide you want to change everything and do it your own way, all those things are not only fine, they can be wonderful. Mistakes in theater can be the most fun part of the whole show as long as you just keep going along and enjoying yourself.

The Sending of Dana Da

(Lights Up. Narrator stands Center Stage.)

NARRATOR: He claimed he was a prophet... sometimes. He claimed he was a wizard ... frequently. He claimed he could tell fortunes ... always. His name was Dana Da, which like everything else about him was a bit of a mystery. When the Englishman Richard Evans saw him again after some years, Dana Da was indeed telling fortunes.

(Dana Da enters and sits Center Stage, the Narrator goes offstage. Richard Evans enters and goes to Dana Da.)

RICHARD: Da, you're telling fortunes now?

DANA DA: One must live, and I am in reduced circumstances.

RICHARD: Well, you must come to my home and have something to eat.

(Dana Da and Richard Evans go to Richard's house, Stage Left, and sit at the table. They eat some of the food.)

DANA DA: Now that you have helped me, how may I help you? Is there anyone you love, for instance, whose love I may help you to obtain?

RICHARD: I can't think of anything. I enjoy my work, I'm in excellent health, and my wife and I already love each other dearly, so I prefer not to drag her into this.

DANA DA: Well, then, is there anyone you hate?

RICHARD: I have to admit there is someone who has so mistreated me as to become my enemy, and has never given me a reason to change my mind.

DANA DA: Excellent. I will dispatch a sending to him. It will absolutely kill him. My own health is sinking fast, but I should like to do this before I go. Because you are my friend, it will cost you only five rupees. What is the name of your enemy?

RICHARD: (Quietly, embarrassed) Everett Lone.

DANA DA: Ahh, I know this man. Once, long ago, he insulted my powers. I should like it to be he.

RICHARD: Look here, Da, I don't want the fellow dead. Couldn't you just . . . well, I don't know, make his life miserable without doing him any real damage?

DANA DA: Ah yes, but that is more expensive than killing him. It takes greater control, you see. That will cost you ten rupees. I am not what I once was, and sadly I must take the money.

(Richard Evans gives Dana Da money. Dana Da spreads out his rug, lies down, moans a few times, goes stiff, then sneezes, then sighs. He sits up.)

DANA DA: The sending has begun. Everett Lone hates cats. Therefore, the sending will take the form of cats. We must send him a letter saying that because he has insulted you and doubted me, a power is directed against him, and soon after he will learn that we speak the truth.

(Dana and Richard exit, the Narrator comes back to Center Stage. As the Narrator talks, Everett Lone enters and sits in his chair, reading the letter. When the narrator says "The servant rushed in" the servant should rush in.)

NARRATOR: Richard Evans promised more money if the sending came to anything. Then he sent a letter to Everett Lone, dictated by Dana Da, warning in most mysterious terms that something was about to happen. In fact, the letter was so vague and so mysterious that it didn't make much sense, which made it seem even more important. After he got it, Everett Lone read it over several times and was still in the process of trying to figure out what it meant when his servant rushed in.

SERVANT: Sir, there is a cat in your bed!

(Everett jumps up; they both walk to the bed. The servant shows Everett the cat.)

EVERETT: Take it away, then change my bed linens. And see to it that this doesn't happen again!

SERVANT: Yes sir.

(Everett sits in his chair.)

NARRATOR: But that night as he was reading in his favorite chair, Everett Lone saw a movement out of the corner of his eye just outside the circle of lamp light. Then, again, he heard "Meow."

EVERETT: Servant!

(The servant comes in and removes the cat from behind the chair.)

EVERETT: How did this thing get here?

SERVANT: I promise, sir, it was not here when I came to turn on your lamp. Besides, real kittens don't stray far from their mothers. There is no mother cat here, so how could these two kittens be real?

EVERETT: Take it away!

(Everett gets up. A guest enters as the narrator continues.)

NARRATOR: The next day as Everett Lone was telling his story to a friend, he was interrupted by a noise among the picture frames on his mantle. It was another kitten, and it knocked the clock onto the floor.

(The servant enters and takes away another kitten from one of the places you have hidden one.)

NARRATOR: Lone and his friend sat down and sent a rather nasty note to Richard Evans telling him in no uncertain terms what they thought of him. When Richard Evans received it, he didn't understand.

(Everett and guest exit, Richard and Dana enter Stage Left. They read the letter. It can be the same letter you used earlier.)

DANA DA: You see? That is my sending. I told you it would work. Give me another ten rupees, if you please.

RICHARD: But Da, what does it mean?

DANA DA: It means cats . . . cats . . . . cats! And more cats! I will send a hundred cats, no, a thousand cats! Ten thousand! This sending will make me famous!

(Richard and Dana exit. As the Narrator speaks, the Servant and Everett Lone enter Stage Right. Everett sits in his chair and looks upset while the Servant runs around and collects some of the kittens.)

NARRATOR: On one point however it appeared that Dana Da was right; when a man who hates cats opens a drawer and discovers one among his socks, finds one sticking its head out of his pajama pocket, or above the rim of his boot, hears a telltale "Meow" from under his chair during dinner, then wakes up one morning with a kitten on his chest, and above all when there's no logical explanation, it's enough to get on his nerves. Everett Lone's eyes grew red from lack of sleep. His voice went up half an octave, and every little noise made him jump. He was not having fun.

(As the Narrator keeps talking, the Servant and Everett exit and Richard and Dana re-enter Stage Left with a letter, which can still be the same one.)

NARRATOR: At the same time, another player entered the story. This was the local wizard, who was furious to hear that someone else was successfully practicing his same business in his territory. Afraid that his customers would begin to go to this newcomer for their services, he began to tell them that it was he, not Dana Da, who was responsible for the sending that everyone had now heard of, thanks to a word dropped by Everett Lone's servant. The wizard wrote a letter to Dana Da claiming all the credit for himself.

DANA DA: So, that is the old man's game, is it? Then the time has come. Write what I tell you, but first give me ten more rupees, please.

(Richard gives him more money.)

DANA DA: Write this: If this is your work, let the sending go on, but if it be mine, let it stop in two more days. On that day, there will be 12 kittens. Twelve! And then no more. Let the people judge between us.

(Richard and Dana exit, Everett re-enters and sits in his chair, and while the Narrator talks, the guests should enter and run around collecting the rest of the kittens, including the ones in the audience.)

NARRATOR: On the specified day, it seemed that half the English population of the city "happened to drop by" Everett Lone's home. Clearly they were curious. Sure enough, kittens began to appear first thing in the morning, and continued throughout the day, and none of the English gentry could believe it. Three kittens showed up in the bathrooms, two were found playing on the rug in front of the hearth, and the others turned up in all sorts of odd places.

GUEST 1: I say, Lone, what's that behind that potted plant?

GUEST 2: Look what I found in your entry hall as I was coming in, old man!

GUEST 3: Good heavens! There's a kitten in my teacup!

(As the Narrator speaks, Everett Lone and all the guests exit, Richard Evans and Dana Da re-enter Stage Left. Dana should lie down on his rug, Richard should kneel next to him.)

NARRATOR: Well of course it was just as Dana Da had predicted in his letter. The old wizard was disgraced, while Everett Lone, who could stand it no longer, packed up and left town. However, Dana Da himself was rapidly headed on an even longer journey. He lay dying in the spare bedroom of Richard Evans' home, where Evans had brought him in his concern. Da had little energy to celebrate his great victory.

DANA DA: The sending is done, but the effort has killed me.

RICHARD: Nonsense. I am afraid you are dying, but the rest is simply not true. Tell me honestly now, how did you do it?

DANA DA: You gave me ten rupees several times, and each time I simply paid Lone's servant two for placing cats, little cats, all over his house. There are no more cats left in the marketplace.

(Dana Da closes his eyes and "dies." Richard stands up, then sits at the table.)

NARRATOR: Afterwards, Richard Evans never told the secret. Dana Da's reputation never suffered, and Everett Lone never returned. And in the years that followed, whenever Richard Evans would think back, he always found himself smiling at the sheer, gorgeous simplicity behind the sending of Dana Da.

(Lights Down, then Lights Up so you can all bow—and maybe throw some kittens at your audience.)